For Victoria, Flinn, Freya and Nat
G.A.

For Melanie, Gerry, Jack and Luke
V.C.

ORCHARD BOOKS
96 Leonard Street, London EC2A 4XD
*Orchard Books Australia*
Unit 31/56 O'Riordan Street, Alexandria NSW 2015
First published in Great Britain in 2001
ISBN 1 84121 313 6
Text © Purple Enterprises 2001
Illustrations © Vanessa Cabban 2001
The rights of Giles Andreae to be identified as the author and
Vanessa Cabban to be identified as the illustrator of this work
have been asserted by them in accordance with the
Copyright, Designs and Patents Act, 1988.
A CIP catalogue record for this book is available
from the British Library
2 3 4 5 6 7 8 9 10
Printed in Singapore

# There's a HOUSE inside my MUMMY

written by
Giles Andreae

illustrated by
Vanessa Cabban

ORCHARD BOOKS

There's a house inside my Mummy
Where my little brother grows,
Or maybe it's my little sister
No-one really knows.

My Daddy says I lived there too
When I was being made,
But I don't remember very much
About it I'm afraid.

He always likes to tell me
It's a lovely place to be,
He knows because he's seen it
On the hospital's T.V.

It's very warm and cosy
But because there's not a bed,
There's a sort of giant bathtub
Where the baby sleeps instead.

He needs to have a lot of room
To help him grow and play,
And that's why Mummy's tummy house
Gets bigger every day.

It's got to have a kitchen
So he doesn't get too thin,
And I think the food my Mummy eats
Can find its way to him.

He seems to want such funny things
But Mummy's very kind,
So she eats all sorts of crazy stuff
And doesn't seem to mind.

I try to help look after her
And see she gets some rest,
Often she falls fast asleep
Before she's got undressed.

Sometimes Mummy feels so sick
I don't know what to do,
But if I had a house in me
I'd feel quite poorly too.

I wish the house had windows
So that we could see inside,
I couldn't find a single one
However hard I tried.

I'd like to show him all my toys
And let him see the view,
And point out all the brilliant things
I'll teach him how to do.

Sometimes me and Mummy
Like to cuddle on our own,
And I tell him that I love him
Through her tummy telephone.

I'm sure that he can hear me
And he likes the way I sound,
'Cause we see him kick his little feet
And somersault around.

I just can't wait to meet him
I hope that he's alright,
My Daddy says be patient
As his door is rather tight.

Look who Mummy made for us -
My lovely little brother!
There's no-one in her tummy now...
UNTIL SHE MAKES ANOTHER!